To
Olivia,
Merry Christmas!
Love,

MoMohins

'Twas the night before Christmas,
when all through the house,
Not a creature was stirring,
not even a mouse;
Olivia's stocking was hung
by the chimney with care,
In hope that St. Nicholas
soon would be there.

Olivia was nestled all snug in her bed,
While visions of candy canes danced in her head.
And Mom in her kerchief, and Dad in his cap,
Had just settled down for a long winter's nap.

When out on the street
there arose such a clatter,
Olivia sprang from her bed—
what was the matter?
Away to the window
Olivia flew like a flash,
Tore open the curtains,
threw open the latch.

The moon on the blanket
of new-fallen snow,
Shone bright as midday
on the objects below—

To
Olivia

When, what to Olivia's
wondering eyes should appear,
But a miniature sleigh
and eight tiny reindeer.

With a little old driver,
so lively and quick,
Olivia knew
that it must be St. Nick.
More rapid than eagles
his reindeer they came,
And he whistled, and shouted,
and called them by name:

To
Olivia

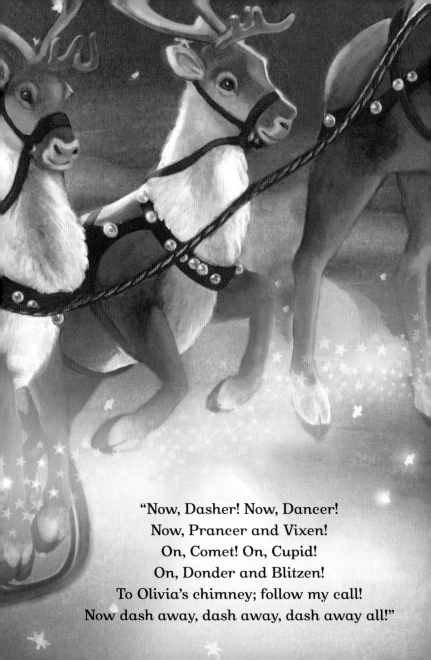

"Now, Dasher! Now, Dancer!
Now, Prancer and Vixen!
On, Comet! On, Cupid!
On, Donder and Blitzen!
To Olivia's chimney; follow my call!
Now dash away, dash away, dash away all!"

Then, in a twinkling,
Olivia heard on the roof
The prancing and pawing
of each little hoof.

Olivia pulled in her head
and was turning around,
When down the chimney
St. Nicholas came with a bound.

He was dressed all in fur,
from his head to his foot,
And his clothes were all tarnished
with ashes and soot.
A bundle of toys he had
flung on his back,
And he looked like a peddler
holding his pack.

To
Olivia

His eyes—how they twinkled!
His dimples—how merry!
His cheeks were like roses,
his nose like a cherry.
His droll little mouth
was drawn up like a bow,
And the beard on his chin was
as white as the snow.

Dear Santa,
I hope you enjoy
the sweet treats.
Love,
Olivia
P.S. The carrots
are for your
furry friends.

A big sack of toys
he held tight in his fist,
He glanced to see Olivia
on top of his list.
He had a broad face
and a little round belly
That shook when he laughed,
like a bowl full of jelly.

Olivia

NICE LIST
Olivia
Jane
Stacey
Elana
Lola

He was chubby and plump,
a right jolly old elf,
And Olivia laughed,
in spite of herself.

A wink of his eye
and a twist of his head,
Let Olivia know
she had nothing to dread.

He spoke not a word,
but went straight to his work,
Filled Olivia's stocking,
then turned with a jerk.

Olivia

And tapping his finger at the side of his nose,
And giving a nod, up the chimney he rose.

He sprang to his sleigh, to his team gave a whistle,
And away they all flew like the down of a thistle.
But St. Nicholas exclaimed, as he drove out of sight—